Published by Modern Publishing,
A Division of Unisystems, Inc.

THE GIGGLEMAJIGS™
Willy and Nilly in
A SQUARE DEAL

Written by Stephen Mooser
Pictures by Frank Hill

MODERN PUBLISHING
A Division of Unisystems, Inc.
New York, New York 10022

One day, the Gigglemajigs, Willy and Nilly, saw a sign in the window of the Square Deal General Store. The sign said:
Solve a Shape Puzzle and Win a Prize!
"Would you like to try solving the puzzle?" asked the store owner, Miss Peeper.
"Yes, please!" said Nilly.
"We're shape experts!" said Willy, as they all went inside.

"This is the puzzle board," said Miss Peeper. "The puzzle pieces are hidden all around the store. You must find them in order to solve the puzzle."

"That should be easy!" cried Willy. "What's the prize, Miss Peeper?"

"A special treat," she said. "But first you must solve the puzzle."

"Let's find the triangle first," said Nilly.
"Found it already!" said Willy.
"Let go of my hat!" cried a customer.

PIZZA

PETS

TRIANGLE

"Now I've found it," Willy said. "A tasty triangle!"

"Here is the puzzle triangle," said Nilly.

"Now let's find the rectangle," said Nilly.
"It's right here!" said Willy. "It's awfully heavy!"
"Put that door back!" cried Miss Peeper.

"Oh, here's the right rectangle!" said Willy.

"Mama!" cried the baby. "He took my book!"

Nilly returned the book to the baby. "And here is the puzzle rectangle, Willy," she said.

RECTANGLE

"Time to find the square," said Nilly.
"I've got it already!" said Willy.
"Hey!" cried the checkers players.

"Look, Willy!" cried Nilly. "The square is on the TV!"

"I don't see a square on TV," said Willy.

"No!" giggled Nilly. "I mean the square is on top of the TV set!"

SQUARE

"I see two circles!" said Willy.

"They're my glasses!" squawked the shopper.

"Here's a nice circle!" said Willy, pointing to a stool.
"But, Willy," Nilly said. "Look underneath the
stool! There's the puzzle circle."

CIRCLE

TRIANGLE

SQUARE

RECTANGLE

CIRCLE

"We solved the puzzle!" cried the Gigglemajigs. "Hooray!"

"Congratulations," said Miss Peeper. "Here's your prize—a box of Snack Time Shaped Cookies."

"Look!" said Willy. "A triangle, a rectangle, and a circle."

"And a square!" Nilly said. "Today sure is shaping up to be lots of fun!"